The Lost
Narwhal

To Patrick, for your endless support of my dreams.

The artwork for this book was created using pencils and digital media.

Designed by Roksolana Panchyshyn

ISBN 978-1-7339196-0-9

www.toriashleymcgee.com

The Lost
Narwhal

by Tori McGee

illustrated by Roksolana Panchyshyn

In the frigid Arctic Ocean,

deep beneath its icy shell,

lives a great majestic creature

who goes by the name of Mel.

Mel's a playful narwhal
with a pointy spiral tusk.
All day long he chases fish,
diving from dawn to dusk.

Mel and the other narwhals
have friendly sing-a-longs.
As they explore the Arctic Circle
they sing lots of narwhal songs.

They sing songs of friendship,
making up tunes as they go.
They whistle spirited melodies,
putting on a joyful show.

Early in the morning,

before anyone's around,

Mel often wanders solo

to nearby Lancaster Sound.

One day as he is roaming
on an adventure all alone,
he finds he's lost his way,
two thousand miles from home!

Mel gets himself all turned around,
darkness falls and the moon's just a sliver.
Realizing he won't make it home for the night,
he settles in on the St. Lawrence River.

While traveling the area
searching for delicious cod,
he spots something downriver.
It's a great beluga pod!

Mel stays off in the distance,

far too nervous to approach them.

What would these new whales think?

Would they even bother with him?

Soon one member of the pod
observes Mel's shy demeanor.
Being an outgoing whale,
she decides to be the greeter.

"Hi, my name is Penny,"
she says with a sweet smile.
"It seems you're far from home.
Come swim with us a while."

Mel follows Penny to her friends,
joining the beluga pod.
As they glide on down the river,
Mel feels a little odd.

Mel notices he's different
from this new beluga crew.
Still he tags along beside them,
doing what the others do.

The belugas also sing songs
just like Mel's narwhal herd.
But these are all new jingles
and Mel doesn't know a word.

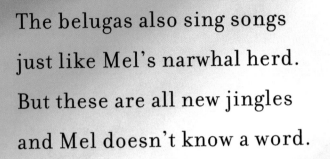

"I used to sing all sorts of songs!"
This thought to Mel occurred.
"I want to join and sing along,
but I'm feeling quite awkward."

Mel confides in Penny

that he's feeling out of place.

He thought that he might just blend in,

but that is not the case.

It's clear that he looks different
even though he fits in well.
Penny understands the songs
are just part of what's troubling Mel.

"Don't worry, Mel," says Penny.

"I'll help you find the beat.

And as for being different,

I think that's what makes you neat!"

Each day Mel and Penny
practice singing a new song.
Mel's grateful that she's patient
when he gets the words all wrong.

Each night when they finish,
Mel hums a narwhal tune.
It comforts him to think of home
beneath the bright blue moon.

One day while swimming with the group,

Mel hears a familiar rhythm.

It's the narwhal song he sings!

They've learned it to sing with him!

The belugas are like family;

Mel feels comfortable with them.

When the whales all get together,

Mel the narwhal fits right in.

But as weeks turn into months,
Mel just can't forget his home.
He wonders when he'll see his friends
in the ocean where they roam.

Penny says she'll search with Mel
to find his narwhal crew.
But what the pair doesn't know
is that his friends are searching too!

The narwhals journey south;

they have a long-lost friend to find.

Mel and Penny head north

to find the home Mel left behind.

About halfway between both homes,
Mel spots a familiar mate.
"Penny! Look! My friends!" he says,
somewhere in the Davis Strait.

The time has come to say goodbye;
their journey is at its end.
Mel didn't know when he set out
what he'd learn from his new friend.

Mel learned a lesson in confidence —
being comfortable in his skin.
He also learned that standing out
doesn't keep you from fitting in.

They each returned back to their homes,
two thousand miles apart.
Though divided by their distance,
they're in each other's hearts.

Made in the USA
Middletown, DE
11 February 2021